GUESS
HOW MUCH
I LOVE YOU

To Liz with love,
A.J.

First published 1994 by
Walker Books Ltd, 87 Vauxhall Walk
London SE11 5HJ

This edition including CD published 2006

10 9 8 7 6 5 4 3 2 1

Text © 1994 Sam McBratney
Illustrations © 1994 Anita Jeram

Guess How Much I Love You™ is a registered trademark of
Walker Books Ltd, London

This book has been typeset in Cochin

Printed in China

British Library Cataloguing in Publication Data:
a catalogue record for this book is available from
the British Library

ISBN-13: 978-1-4063-0284-4
ISBN-10: 1-4063-0284-8

www.walkerbooks.co.uk

GUESS HOW MUCH I LOVE YOU

Written by
Sam McBratney

Illustrated by
Anita Jeram

WALKER BOOKS
AND SUBSIDIARIES
LONDON · BOSTON · SYDNEY · AUCKLAND

L̲ittle Nutbrown Hare, who was going to bed, held on tight to Big Nutbrown Hare's very long ears.

He wanted to be sure that Big
Nutbrown Hare was listening.
"Guess how much
I love you," he said.

"Oh, I don't think I could guess that,"
said Big Nutbrown Hare.

"This much," said Little Nutbrown Hare, stretching out his arms as wide as they could go.

Big Nutbrown Hare had even
longer arms. "But I love YOU
this much," he said.

Hmm, that is a lot, thought
Little Nutbrown Hare.

"I love you as high as I can reach," said Little Nutbrown Hare.

"I love you as high as *I* can reach," said Big Nutbrown Hare.

That is quite
high, thought
Little Nutbrown
Hare. I wish
I had arms
like that.

Then Little
Nutbrown Hare
had a good idea.
He tumbled
upside down
and reached
up the tree
trunk with
his feet.

"I love you
all the way up
to my toes!"
he said.

"And *I* love you
all the way up
to your toes," said
Big Nutbrown Hare,
swinging him up
over his head.

"I love you
as high as
I can HOP!"
laughed Little
Nutbrown Hare,

bouncing up
and down.

"But I love you as high as
I can hop," smiled Big
Nutbrown Hare – and he
hopped so high that his ears
touched the branches above.

That's good
hopping,
thought
Little
Nutbrown
Hare.
I wish I
could hop
like that.

"I love you all the way down the lane as far as the river," cried Little Nutbrown Hare.

"I love you across the river
and over the hills," said
Big Nutbrown Hare.

That's very far, thought
Little Nutbrown Hare.

He was almost too sleepy
to think any more.

Then he looked beyond the
thorn bushes, out into the big
dark night. Nothing could
be further than the sky.

"I love you right up to
the MOON," he said,
and closed his eyes.

"Oh, that's far," said
Big Nutbrown Hare.
"That is very,
very far."

Big Nutbrown Hare settled
Little Nutbrown Hare
into his bed of leaves.

He leaned over
and kissed him
good night.

Then he lay down close by
and whispered with a smile,
"I love you right up to the moon –

AND BACK."